Thomas Augustine Arne, William Mason

Caractacus

A dramatic poem

Thomas Augustine Arne, William Mason

Caractacus
A dramatic poem

ISBN/EAN: 9783337393540

Printed in Europe, USA, Canada, Australia, Japan

Cover: Foto ©Andreas Hilbeck / pixelio.de

More available books at **www.hansebooks.com**

CARACTACUS.

A

DRAMATIC POEM.

Written on the Model of

The ANTIENT GREEK TRAGEDY.

First publifhed in the Year 1759, .

A N D.

Now altered for Theatrical Reprefentation.

By W. MASON, M.A.

NOS MUNERA PHOEBO
MISIMUS, ET LECTAS DRUIDUM DE GENTE CHOREAS.
MILTON.

Y O R K :

Printed by A. WARD; and fold by R. HORSFIELD and
J. DODSLEY, in London.

M DCC LXXVII.

[Price One Shilling and Six-Pence.]

TO THE RIGHT REVEREND THE BISHOP
OF LICHFIELD AND COVENTRY, PRE-
CEPTOR TO THEIR ROYAL HIGHNESSES
THE PRINCE OF WALES AND BISHOP
OF OSNABRUG.

S O N N E T.

STILL let my HURD a fmile of candour lend
To Scenes, that dar'd on Grecian pennons tower,
When *, " in low Thurcafton's fequefter'd bower,"
He prais'd the ftrain, becaufe he lov'd the friend :
There golden Leifure did his fteps attend,
Nor had the rare, yet well-weigh'd, call of Power
To thofe high cares decreed his watchful hour,
On which fair ALBION's future hopes depend.
A Fate unlook'd for waits my Friend and me ;
He pays to duty what was learning's claim,
Refigning claffic eafe for dignity ;
I yield my Mufe to Fafhion's praife or blame :
Yet ftill our hearts in this great truth agree,
That Peace alone is blifs, and Virtue fame.

Afton, Nov. 12, 1776.   W. M A S O N.

* See the conclufion of an Elegy prefixed to the former
Editions of this Poem.

LETTER to THOMAS HARRIS, Efq;

SIR,

YOUR very fair and candid behaviour towards me, in not only afking my permiffion to bring CARACTACUS upon the Stage, but in thinking me capable of making the Alterations in it, requifite for that purpofe, is fo flattering and unexpected an inftance of condefcenfion in the Manager of a Theatre, that it not only demands my beft acknowledgments, but has induced me very readily to give up a few of my leifure hours to the attempt.

As I have endeavoured, in fitting it for the Stage, not to leave it totally unfit for the Clofet, I fufpect it may ftill be too long for reprefentation. If, therefore, upon Rehearfal with the Mufic, you fhould find this to be the cafe, I will fend you a fecond Copy, in which feveral other lines and paffages fhall be mark'd with inverted commas, which you may either omit, or retain, as fhall then feem expedient. But, if I print the Tragedy, thefe paffages will not be fo marked, for the above reafon.

If I wifh for the fuccefs of my Poem, in this form, I affure you, Sir, it is chiefly on your account, that you may not fuffer by the very great expence which you intend to be at in the exhibition.

Believe me to be, with very true regard,

SIR,

Your moft obedient

Sept. 10, 1776.

and faithful Servant,

W. MASON.

PERSONS of the DRAMA.

Caractacus, King of the Silures	Mr. Clarke.
Aulus Didius, the Roman General	Mr. Whitfield.
Arviragus, Son to Caractacus ——	Mr. Lewis.
Vellinus, ⎫ Sons to Cartifmandua	Mr. Ward.
Elidurus, ⎭ Queen of the Brigantes.	Mr. Wroughton.
Evelina, Daughter to Caractacus —	Mrs. Hartley.

PERSONS of the CHORUS.

Modred, the chief Druid ——	Mr. Aikin.
Mador *, the chief Bard ——	Mr. Hull.
Second Bard —— ——	Mr. Leoni.
Third Bard — —— ——	Mrs. Farrel.
Fourth Bard —— ——	Mr. Reinold.

Scene, the confecrated Grove in the Ifland of Mona,
now Anglefea.

* Thofe parts only of the Odes which are printed in Italics,
are meant to be performed mufically, the reft to be recited by
the chief Bard.

CARACTACUS.

ACT I.

SCENE I.

AULUS DIDIUS, *with Romans.*

THIS is the fecret centre of the ifle:
　Here, Romans, paufe, and let the eye of wonder
Gaze on the folemn fcene; behold yon oak
How ftern he frowns, and with his broad brown arms
Chills the pale plain beneath him: mark yon altar,
The dark ftream brawling round its rugged bafe,
Thefe cliffs, thefe yawning caverns, this wide circus,
Skirted with unhewn ftone: they awe my foul.
Surely, my friends, there is a hidden power
In the lone majefty of untam'd nature,
Controuling fober reafon; tell me elfe,
Why do thefe haunts of barb'rous fuperftition
O'ercome me thus? I fcorn them, yet they awe me.
Call forth the Britifh Princes: in this gloom
I mean to fchool them to our enterprize.

SCENE II.

AULUS DIDIUS, VELLINUS, ELIDURUS.

Ye pledges dear of CARTISMANDUA's faith,
Approach! and to my uninftructed ear
Explain this fcene of horror.

A

E L I-

ELIDURUS.

Daring Roman,
Know that thou ftand'ft on confecrated ground :
Thefe mighty piles of magic-planted rock,
Thus rang'd in myftic order, mark the place
Where but at times of holieft feftival
The Druid leads his train.

AULUS DIDIUS.

Where dwells the feer?

VELLINUS.

In yonder fhaggy cave; on which the moon
Now fheds a fide-long gleam. His brotherhood
Poffefs the neighb'ring cliffs.

AULUS DIDIUS.

Yet up the hill
Mine eye defcries a diftant range of caves,
Delv'd in the ridges of the craggy fteep :
And this way ftill another.

ELIDURUS.

On the left
Refide the fage EUVATES: yonder grots
Are tenanted by Bards, who nightly thence,
Rob'd in their flowing vefts of innocent white,
Defcend, with harps that glitter to the moon,
Hymning immortal ftrains. The fpirits of air,
Of earth, of water, nay of heav'n itfelf,
Do liften to their lay. Now if thy eye
Be fated with the view, hafte to thy fhips;
And ply thine oars; for, if the Druids learn
This bold intrufion, thou wilt find it hard
To foil their fury.

AULUS DIDIUS.

Prince, I did not moor
My light-arm'd fhallops on this dangerous ftrand
To footh a fruitlefs curiofity :
I come in queft of proud CARACTACUS;

Who,

Who, when our veterans put his troops to flight,
Found refuge here.

ELIDURUS.

If here the Monarch rests,
Presumptuous Chief! thou might'st as well essay
To pluck him from yon stars: Beneath the soil
We tread, a hundred dark mysterious paths
Lead to as many caverns, in whose womb
He may for life lie hid.

AULUS DIDIUS.

We know the task
Most difficult: yet has thy royal mother
Furnish'd the means.

ELIDURUS.

My mother, say'st thou, Roman?

AULUS DIDIUS.

In proof of that firm faith she lends to Rome,
She gave you up her honour's hostages.

ELIDURUS.

She did: and we submit.

AULUS DIDIUS.

To Rome we bear you;
From your dear country bear you; from your joys,
Your loves, your friendships, all your souls hold precious.

ELIDURUS.

And dost thou taunt us, Roman, with our fate?

AULUS DIDIUS.

No, youth, by heav'n, I would avert that fate.
Wish ye for liberty?

VELLINUS, ELIDURUS.

More than for life.

AULUS DIDIUS.

And would do much to gain it?

VELLINUS.

Name the task.

A 2   AULUS

A U L U S D I D I U S.

The tafk is eafy. Hafte ye to thefe Druids:
Tell them ye come, commiffion'd by your Queen,
To feek the great CARACTACUS; and call
His valor to her aid. Her truce with Rome
Is yet unknown: and this her royal fignet
Shall be your pledge of faith. The eager king
Will gladly take the charge; and, he confenting,
What elfe remains, but to the Menaï's fhore
Ye lead his credulous ftep? there will we feize him:
Bear him to Rome, the fubftitute for you,
And give you back to freedom.

V E L L I N U S.

If the Druids—

A U L U S D I D I U S.

If they, or he, prevent this artifice,
Then force muft take its way: then flaming brands,
" And biting axes, wielded by our foldiers,"
Muft level thefe thick fhades, and fo unlodge
The lurking favage.

E L I D U R U S

Gods, fhall Mona perifh?

A U L U S D I D I U S.

Princes, her ev'ry trunk fhall on the ground
Stretch its gigantic length; unlefs, ere dawn,
Ye lure this untam'd lion to our toils.
Go then, and profper; I fhall to the fhips,
And there expect his coming. Youths, remember,
He muft to Rome to grace great CÆSAR's triumph:
CÆSAR and Fate demand him at your hand.

[*Exeunt Aulus Didius and Romans.*

SCENE

S C E N E III.

ELIDURUS, VELLINUS.

ELIDURUS.

And will heav'n fuffer it? Will the juft gods,
That tread yon fpangled pavement o'er our heads,
Look from their fky and yield him? Wi'l thefe Druids,
Their fage vicegerents, not call down the thunder
In fuch a righteous caufe? Yes, good old king,
Yes, laft of Britons, thou art heav'n's own pledge;
And fhalt be fuch till death.

VELLINUS.

      What means my brother?
Doft thou refufe the charge?

ELIDURUS.

      Doft thou accept it?

VELLINUS.

It gives us liberty.

ELIDURUS.

     It makes us traitors.
Gods, would VELLINUS do a deed of bafenefs?

VELLINUS.

Will ELIDURUS fcorn the proffer'd boon
Of freedom?

ELIDURUS.

     Yes, when fuch its guilty price,
Brother, I fpurn it.

VELLINUS.

    Go then, foolifh boy!
I'll do the deed myfelf.

ELIDURUS.

     It fhall not be:
I will proclaim the fraud.

VELLINUS.

     Wilt thou? 'tis well.
Hie to yon cave; call loudly on the Druid;

         And

And bid him drag to ignominious death
The partner of thy blood.

ELIDURUS.

O my VELLINUS!
Rend not my foul: by heav'n thou know'ft I love thee,
As fervently as brother e'er lov'd brother:
And, loving thee, I thought I lov'd mine honour.
Ah! do not wake, dear Youth, in this true breaft
So fierce a conflict.

VELLINUS.

Honour's voice commands
Thou fhould'ft obey thy mother, and thy queen.
Honour and Holinefs alike confpire
To bid thee fave thefe confecrated groves
From Roman devaftation.

ELIDURUS.

Horrid thought!
Hence let us hafte, even to the furtheft nook
Of this wide ifle; nor view the facrilege.

VELLINUS.

No, let us ftay, and by our profperous art
Prevent the facrilege. Mark me, my brother;
More years and more experience have matur'd
My fober thought; I will convince thy youth,
That this our deed has ev'ry honeft fanction
Cool reafon may demand.

ELIDURUS.

To Rome with reafon:
Try if 'twill bring her deluging ambition
Into the level courfe of right and juftice.
But, pray thee, do not reafon from my foul
Its inbred honefty: that holy flame,
Howe'er eclips'd by Rome's black influence
In vulgar minds, ought ftill to brighten ours.

VELLINUS.

Vain talker, leave me.

ELI-

E L I D U R U S.

No, I will not leave thee :
I muft not, dare not, in thefe perilous fhades.
Think, if thy fraud fhould fail, thefe holy men,
How will their juftice rend thy trait'rous limbs ?
If thou fucceed'ft, the fiercer pangs of confcience,
How will they ever goad thy guilty foul ?
Mercy, defend us ! fee, the awful Druids
Are iffuing from their caves : hear'ft thou yon fignal ?
Lo, on the inftant all the mountain whitens
With flow-defcending Bards. Retire, retire ;
This is the hour of facrifice : to ftay
Is death.

V E L L I N U S.

I'll wait the clofing of their rites
In yonder vale : do thou, as likes thee beft,
Betray, or aid me.

E L I D U R U S.

To betray thee, youth,
That love forbids ; honour, alas ! to aid thee.

[*Exeunt.*

S C E N E IV.

The CHORUS, *preceded by* MODRED *the chief
Druid, defcend to a folemn Symphony.*

M O D R E D.

Sleep and Silence reign around ;
Not a night-breeze wakes to blow ;
  Circle, fons, this holy ground ;
Circle clofe, in triple row.

C H O R U S.

*Druid, at thy dread command,
When thou wav'ft thy potent wand,*

See,

See, we pace this holy ground
With solemn footsteps soft and slow,
While Sleep and Silence reign around,
And not a night-breeze wakes to blow.

M O D R E D.

'Tis well. And now, if mask'd in vapours drear,
Any malign or earth-born Spirit dare
To hover round this confecrated fpace,
Hafte with light fpells the murky foe to chace.

C H O R U S.

We lift our boughs of vervain blue,
Dipt in cold September dew,
And dash the moifture, chafte and clear,
O'er the ground, and thro' the air.

M O D R E D.

Now the place is purg'd and pure.—[*A fhort Symphony.*
Brethren ! fay, for this high hour,
Are the milk-white fteers prepar'd ?
Whofe necks the rude yoke never fcar'd,
To the furrow yet unbroke ?
For fuch muft bleed beneath yon oak.

C H O R U S.

Druid, thefe, in order meet,
Are all prepar'd.

M O D R E D.

                    But tell me yet,
CADWALL ! did thy ftep profound
Dive into the cavern deep,
Twice twelve fathom under ground,
Where our fage fore-fathers fleep ?
Thence with reverence haft thou born,
From the confecrated cheft,
The golden fickle, fcrip, and veft,
Whilom by old BELINUS worn ?

Second B A R D.

Druid, thefe, in order meet,
Are all prepar'd.

M O D R E D.

But tell me yet,
From the grot of charms and fpells,
Where our matron fifter dwells,
BRENNUS ! has thy holy hand
Safely brought the druid wand;
And the potent adder-ftone,
Gender'd 'fore th' autumnal moon?

Third B A R D.

Druid, thefe, in order meet,
Are all prepar'd.

M O D R E D.

Then all's compleat.

[*Symphony repeated.*

And now let nine of the felected band
With wary circuit pace around the grove,
And guard each inlet; watchful, left the eye
Of bufy curiofity profane
Pry on our rites: for know, CARACTACUS
This night demands admiffion to our train.
He, once our king, while ought his pow'r avail'd
To fave his country from the rod of tyrants,
That duty paft, does wifely now retire
To end his days in fecrecy and peace;
Druid with Druids, in this chief of groves,
Ev'n in the heart of Mona. See, he comes!
How awful is his port! mark him, my friends!
He looks, as doth the tower, whofe nodding walls,
After the conflict of heav'n's angry bolts,
Frown with a dignity unmark'd before,
Ev'n in its prime of ftrength. Health to the king!

B   SCENE

S C E N E V.

CARACTACUS, EVELINA, MODRED, CHORUS.

C A R A C T A C U S.

This holy place, methinks, doth this night wear
More than its wonted gloom : Druid, these groves
Have caught the difmal colouring of my foul
In pity to their gueft.   Hail, hallow'd oaks !
Hail, Britifh born ! who, laft of Britifh race,
Hold your primæval rights by nature's charter ;
Not at the nod of CÆSAR.   Happy forefters,
Ye wave your bold heads in the liberal air ;
Nor afk, for privilege, a prætor's edict.
Ye, with your tough and intertwifted roots,
Grafp the firm rocks ye grew from ; fpreading proudly
Your leafy banners 'gainft the tyrannous north,
Who Roman-like affails you.   Tell me, Druid,
Is it not better to be fuch as thefe,
Than be the thing I am ?

M O D R E D.
                                        To be the thing
Eternal wifdom wills, is ever beft.

C A R A C T A C U S.
But I am loft to that predeftin'd ufe
Eternal wifdom will'd, and fitly therefore
May wifh a change of being.   I was born
A king; and heav'n, who bad thefe warrior oaks
Lift their green fhields againft the fiery fun,
Meant that this arm fhould fo protect my people
Againft the peftilent glare of Rome's ambition.
I fail'd ; and how I fail'd, thou know'ft too well ;
So does the babbling world : and therefore, Druid,
I would be any thing fave what I am.

M O D R E D.
See, to thy wifh, the holy rites prepar'd,

                                                Which,

Which, if heav'n frown not, confecrate thee Druid:
Meanwhile bethink thee, Prince, if ought on earth
Still holds too firm an union with thy foul,
Eftranging it from peace.

CARACTACUS.

      I had a queen:
Bear with my weaknefs, Druid! this tough breaft
Muft heave a figh, for fhe is unreveng'd.
And then can I tafte peace? Ah! EVELINA,
Hang not thus weeping on the feeble arm
That could not fave thy mother.

EVELINA.

      To hang thus
Softens the pang of grief; and the fweet thought,
That a fond father ftill fupports his child,
Sheds, on my penfive mind, fuch foothing balm,
As doth the blefling of thefe pious feers,
When moft they wifh our welfare. Would to heav'n
A daughter's prefence could as much avail
To eafe her father's woes, as his doth mine.

CARACTACUS.

Ever moft gentle! come unto my bofom:
Dear pattern of the precious prize I loft,
Loft, fo inglorious loft; my friends, thefe eyes
Did fee her torn from my defencelefs camp;
Whilft I, hemm'd round by fquadrons, could not fave her:
My boy, ftill nearer to the darling pledge,
Beheld her fhrieking in the ruffian's arm;
Beheld and fled.

EVELINA.

    Ah! Sir, forbear to wound
My brother's fame; he fled, but to recall
His fcatter'd forces to purfue and fave her.

CARACTACUS.

Daughter, he fled. Now, by yon gracious moon,
That rifing faw the deed, and inftant hid

        Her

Her blufhing face in twilight's dufky veil,
The flight was parricide.
EVELINA.
Indeed, indeed,
I know him valiant; and not doubt he fell
'Mid flaughter'd thoufands of the haughty foe,
Victim to filial love. ARVIRAGUS,
Thou had'ft no fifter near the bloody field,
Whofe forrowing fearch, led by yon orb of night,
Might find thy body; wafh with tears thy wounds;
And wipe them with her hair.
MODRED.
Peace, virgin, peace:
Nor thou, fad Prince, reply: whate'er he is,
Be he a captive, fugitive, or corfe,
He is what heav'n ordain'd: thefe holy groves
Permit no exclamation 'gainft heav'n's will
To violate their echoes. Patience, here,
Her meek hands folded on her modeft breaft,
In mute fubmiffion lifts th' adoring eye,
Ev'n to the ftorm that wrecks her.
EVELINA.
Holy Druid,
If ought my erring tongue has faid pollutes
This facred place, I from my foul abjure it.
And will thefe lips bar with eternal filence,
Rather than fpeak a word, or act a deed,
Unmeet for thy fage daughters; bleffing firft
This hallow'd hour that takes me from the world,
And joins me to their fober fifterhood.
MODRED.
'Tis wifely faid. See, Prince, this prudent maid,
Now, while the ruddy flame of fparkling youth
Glows on her beauteous cheek, can quit the world
Without a figh, whilft thou————

CARAC-

CARACTACUS.

Would fave my queen
From a bafe ravifher; would wifh to plunge
This falchion in his breaft, and fo avenge
Infulted royalty. O holy men!
Ye are the fons of piety and peace;
Ye never felt the fharp vindictive fpur
That goads the injur'd warrior, elfe indeed
Ye much would pity me; would curfe the fate
That coops me here inactive in your groves,
Robs me of hope, tells me this trufty fteel
Muft never cleave one Roman helm again;
Never avenge my queen, nor free my country.

MODRED.

'Tis heaven's high will——

CARACTACUS.

I know it, reverend fathers!
'Tis heav'n's high will that thefe poor aged eyes
Shall never more behold that virtuous woman,
To whom my youth was conftant; 'twas heav'n's will
To take her from me at that very hour,
When beft her love might footh me; that black hour,
[May memory ever raze it from her records]
When all my fquadrons fled, and left their king
Old and defencelefs: him, who nine whole years,
Had taught them how to conquer: yes, my friends,
For nine whole years againft the fons of rapine
I led my veterans, oft to victory,
Never 'till then to fhame. Bear with me, Druid,
I've done: begin the rites.

MODRED.

No. We poftpone
Thofe rites, vain Prince! 'till Refignation meek,
'Till dove-ey'd Peace, hand-maid of Sanctity,
Approach this altar with thee. Bards, bear off
The victims. No reply. A frame of mind,

More

More fitted to thefe rites, muft Patience bring
To give them holy fanction. Thefe inftead,
See I not gaunt Revenge, enfanguin'd Slaughter,
And mad Ambition, clinging to thy foul,
Eager to fnatch thee back to their domain,
Back to a vain and miferable world;
Whofe mifery and vanity, tho' try'd,
Thou ftill hold'ft dearer than thefe folemn fhades,
Where Quiet reigns with Virtue? Try we yet
That gradual aid which Holinefs can lend,
For much it can, by preparation meet
Of fage myfterious office: " when the foul,
Snatch'd by the pow'r of mufic from her cell
Of flefhly thraldom, feels herfelf upborn
On plumes of extafy, and boldly fprings
'Mid fwelling harmonies and pealing hymns,
Up to the porch of heav'n. Strike, then, ye Bards!
Strike all your ftrings fymphonious; wake a ftrain
Which, as it echoes thro' yon vaulted cave,
May penetrate, may purge, may purify,
His yet unhallow'd bofom. To that cave,
Monarch, retire, while hither we invoke
The airy tribe that on yon mountain dwell,
Ev'n on majeftic Snowdon: they, who never
Deign vifit mortal men, fave on fome caufe
Of higheft import, but, fublimely fhrin'd
On its hoar top in domes of cryftalline ice,
Hold converfe with thofe fpirits that poffefs
The fky's pure fapphire, neareft heav'n itfelf.

[*Exeunt Caractacus & Evelina.*

SCENE

SCENE VI.

MADOR, CHORUS.

O D E.   *[Symphony.*

MADOR.

Mona on Snowdon calls.

CHORUS.

Hear, thou King of mountains, hear;
Hark, she speaks from all her strings;
Hark, her loudest echo rings;
King of mountains, bend thine ear.

MADOR.

Send thy spirits, send them soon,
Now, when Midnight and the Moon
Meet upon thy front of snow:
   See, their gold and ebon rod,
   Where the sober sisters nod,
And greet in whispers sage and slow.   *[Symphony.*
Snowdon mark ! 'tis Magic's hour;
Now the mutter'd spell hath pow'r;
Pow'r to rend thy ribs of rock,
And burst thy base with thunder's shock:
But to thee no ruder spell
Shall Mona use, than those that dwell
In Music's secret cells, and lie
Steep'd in the stream of Harmony.

AIR by the second BARD.

Snowdon, to thee no ruder spell
Shall Mona use, than those that dwell
In Music's secret cells, and lie
Steep'd in the stream of Harmony.

MADOR,

M A D O R.

Snowdon has heard the ftrain :   [*Symphony.*
Hark, amid the wond'ring grove
  Other harpings anfwer clear,
  Other voices meet our ear,
Pinions flutter, fhadows move.   [*Symphony.*
Bufy murmurs hum around,
Ruftling veftments brufh the ground ;
Round, and round, and round they go,
Thro' the twilight, thro' the fhade,
Mount the oak's majeftic head,
And gild the tufted mifletoe.

D U E T by the fecond and third B A R D S.

  Welcome, welcome, gentle Train,
  Mona hails ye to her plain ;
  Here, your genial dews difpenfe ;
  Dews of Peace, and Innocence.
  Banifh hence each demon drear,
  Fev'rifh Rage, and chilling Fear,
  Vengeance with his haggard eye,
  Envy, Hate, and Jealoufy.

M A D O R.

Mona ! thy grove is Virtue's throne ;
To Peace, to Piety alone
  Thy central Oak its fhade extends ;
Here, melting in Devotion's fires,
The Soul, fublim'd, to heav'n afpires,
  Its drofs fubfides, its gold afcends.
Pure, as this glitt'ring race of light
That tend thy call from Snowdon's height ;
That here, arrang'd in order due,
Spread their bright robes of faffron hue ;
So pure, fo bright, thy fons fhall fhine,
  When life's delufive dream is o'er ;
Like them be crown'd with mifletoe divine,
  Like them in azure fields of Ether foar,

                               Full

Full C H O R U S.

Mona! thy grove is Virtue's throne;
To Peace, to Piety alone
Thy central Oak its shade extends;
Here, melting in Devotion's fires,
The soul, sublim'd, to heav'n aspires,
Its dross subsides, its gold ascends.

END *of the* F I R S T A C T.

C   A C T

ACT II.

SCENE I.

CARACTACUS, MODRED, CHORUS.

CARACTACUS.

TRUST me, thou fire of Mona! All my foul
    Is now prepar'd. I feel as fhould the man
Who, fcorning what he was, who, what he is,
Lamenting, refts all future hope of peace
On what thy rites fhall make him. Holy Druid,
Recall thy word; give fignal for thofe rites.

MODRED.

The cuftom'd hour is paft. It may not be.
What yet remains of night we dedicate
To pious mufing. Be thy ftation, Prince,
Behind the altar; and, if fleep fhould deign
There to defcend upon thy clofed lids,
Haply her opiate poppies may fupply
More than their wonted balm, and purge thy foul
From each remaining frailty. Many there,
Refting their heads, have had experience ftrange
Of influential fanctity convey'd
In dream or vifion, whofe protracted power,
Full long beyond that dream or vifion's date,
Remain'd to blefs their bofoms.——Whence that
    noife?
Methought I heard the found of fteps profane.
Monarch, retire, the central Oak doth fhake.

[Exit Caractacus.

Enter a BARD.

Father, as we did watch the eaftern fide,
We faw, and inftant feiz'd two ftranger youths,
Who in the bottom of a fhadowy dell,

Held

Held earneſt converſe. Britons do they ſeem,
And of Brigantian race.
M O D R E D.
Haſte, drag them hither.

S C E N E II.

VELLINUS, ELIDURUS, MODRED, CHORUS.

V E L L I N U S.
O ſpare, ye ſage and venerable Druids,
Your countrymen and ſons,
M O D R E D.
And are ye Britons?
Unheard of profanation! Rome herſelf
Would not have dar'd ſo raſhly.   Oh! for words,
Big with the fierceſt force of execration,   .
To blaſt the deed and doers.
E L I D U R U S.
Spare the curſe,
Oh! ſpare our youth!
M O D R E D.
Is it not now the hour,
The holy hour, when to the cloudleſs height
Of yon ſtarr'd concave climbs the full-orb'd moon,
And to this nether world in ſolemn ſtillneſs
Gives ſign, that to the liſt'ning ear of Heav'n
Religion's voice ſhould plead? The very babe
Knows this, and, chance awak'd, his little hands
Liſts to the Gods, and on his innocent couch
Calls down a bleſſing.   Learn ye, wretches, learn,
At ſuch an hour to preſs this hallow'd plain
Is ſacrilege.
V E L L I N U S.
Dread Seer! were Mona's plain
More hallow'd ſtill, hallow'd as is Heav'n's ſelf,
The cauſe might plead our pardon.
E L I-

ELIDURUS.

Mighty Druid!
True, we have rafhly dar'd, yet forc'd by duty,
Our fov'reign's mandate——

VELLINUS.

Elder by my birth,
Brother, I claim, in right of elderfhip,
To open our high embaffy.

MODRED.

Speak then;
But fee thy words anfwer in honeft weight
To this proud prelude. Youth! they muft be weighty,
T' atone for fuch a crime.

VELLINUS.

If then to give
New nerves to vanquifh'd valour; if to fave
A bleeding country from oppreffion's fword,
Be weighty bufinefs, know, that bufinefs ours.

MODRED.

Declare it then at once, briefly and boldly.

VELLINUS.

CARACTACUS is here.

MODRED.

Say'ft thou, proud boy ?
Tis boldly faid, and, grant 'twere truly faid,
Think'ft thou he were not here from fraud or force
As fafe as in a camp of conquerors ?
Here, youth, he would be guarded by the Gods;
Each hair of his bleft head would in thefe caverns
Sleep with the unfunn'd filver of the mine,
As precious and as fafe; record the time,
When Mona e'er betray'd the haplefs wretch,
That made her groves his refuge.

VELLINUS.

Holy Druid!
Can force, alas! dwell in our unarm'd hands?

Can

Can fraud in our young bofoms? Know, dread Seer,
We are the fons of her whofe righteous fway
Bleffes the bold Brigantes; men who firmly
Have three long moons withftood th' affailing pow'rs
Of fell Ostorius, that now falcon-like
Hang o'er our heads fufpended. Such the ftate
Of us and Rome; in which our prudent mother
Sends us to feek the great CARACTACUS,
Calling his valour forth to lead her bands,
To fight the caufe of Liberty and Britain,
And quell thefe ravagers.

[*Caraƈtacus ftarts from behind the altar.*

S C E N E III.

CARACTACUS, MODRED, VELLINUS, ELIDURUS, CHORUS.

C A R A C T A C U S.

                    And ye have found me;
Friends, ye have found me: bring me to your Queen,
And the laft purple drop in thefe old veins
Shall fall for her and Britain.

M O D R E D.

                    Rafh, rafh Prince!

V E L L I N U S.

Ye bleft immortal powers! is this the man,
The more than man, who for nine bloody years
Withftood all Rome? He is; that warlike front,
Seam'd o'er with honeft fcars, proclaims he is:
Kneel, brother, kneel, while in his royal hand
We lodge the fignet: this, in pledge of faith,
Great CARTISMANDUA fends, and with it tells thee
She has a nobler pledge than this behind;
Thy Queen——

C A R A C T A C U S.
GUIDERIA!

                              V E L-

VELLINUS.

Safely with our Mother.

CARACTACUS.

How, when, where refcu'd? mighty Gods, I thank ye,
For it is true, this fignet fpeaks it true.
O tell me briefly.

VELLINUS.

In a fally, Prince,
Which, wanting abler chiefs, my gracious mother
Committed to my charge, our troops affail'd
One outwork of the camp; and there my hand
Was doom'd with other prifoners to releafe
The captive matron.

CARACTACUS.

Let me clafp thee, youth,
And thou fhalt be my fon: I had one, ftranger,
Juft of thy years; he look'd like thee right honeft;
And yet he fail'd me. Were it not for him,
Who, as thou feeft, ev'n at this hour of joy,
Draws tears down mine old cheek, I were as bleft
As the great Gods. Oh, he has all difgrac'd
His high-born anceftry! But I'll forget him.
Hafte, EVELINA, barb my knotty fpear,
My bow, my target———

MODRED.

Rafh CARACTACUS!
What haft thou done? What doft thou mean to do?

CARACTACUS.

To fave my country.

MODRED.

To betray thyfelf.
That thou haft done; the reft thou canft not do,
If Heav'n forbids; and of its will thou recks not.
Say, when thefe youths approach'd, did not the Oak,
That fhades yon Altar, tremble? fuch an omen
Might bid thee doubt their truth.

CARAC-

CARACTACUS.
                          By Heav'n, I feel,
Beyond all omens, that within my breaft,
Which marfhals me to conqueft; fomething here
That fnatches me beyond all mortal fears,
Lifts me to where upon her jafper throne
Sits flame-rob'd Victory, who calls me fon,
And crowns me with a Palm, whofe deathlefs green
Shall bloom when CÆSAR's fades.

MODRED.
                          Vain confidence!

CARACTACUS.
Yet I fubmit in all——

MODRED.
                    'Tis meet thou fhould'ft.
Thou art a King, a fov'reign o'er frail man;
I am a Druid, fervant of the Gods;
Such fervice is above fuch fov'reignty,
As well thou know'ft: if they fhould prompt thefe lips
To interdict the thing thou dar'ft to do,
What would avail thy daring?

CARACTACUS.
                          Holy man!
But thou wilt blefs it; Heav'n will bid thee blefs it;
Thou know'ft that, when we fight to fave our country,
We fight the caufe of Heav'n. The man that falls,
Falls hallow'd; falls a victim for the Gods;
For them and for their altars.

MODRED.
                          Valiant Prince!
Think not we lightly rate our country's weal,
Or thee, our country's champion. Well we know
The glorious meed of thofe exalted fouls,
Who flame like thee for freedom: mark me, Prince!
The time will come, when Deftiny and Death,
Thron'd in a burning car, the thund'ring wheels
                                        Arm'd

Arm'd with gigantic fcythes of adamant,
Shall fcour this field of life: and in the rear
The fiend Oblivion: kingdoms, empires, worlds
Melt in the general blaze: when, lo! from high
Andrafte darting, catches from the wreck
The roll of Fame, claps her afcending plumes,
And ftamps on orient ftars each patriot name,
Round her eternal dome.

C A R A C T A C U S.

Speak ever thus,
And I will hear thee, 'till attention faint
In heedlefs extafy.

M O D R E D.

This tho' we know,
Let man beware with headlong zeal to rufh
Where flaughter calls; it is not courage, Prince!
No nor the pride and practis'd fkill in arms,
That gains this meed: the warrior is no patriot,
Save when, obfequious to the will of Heav'n,
He draws the fword of vengeance.

C A R A C T A C U S.

Surely, Druid,
Such fair occafion fpeaks the will of Heav'n ————

M O D R E D.

Monarch, perchance thou haft a fair occafion:
But, if thou haft, the Gods will foon declare it:
And this demands our fearch. Mortals, retire!
Leave ye the grove to us and Infpiration.

[*Exeunt Caractacus, Vellinus, &c.*

S C E N E IV.

M O D R E D, C H O R U S.

M O D R E D.

My holy Brethren ftay; and you, ye Bards,
LEOLINE, CADWALL, HOEL, CANTABER,

Attend

Attend upon our slumbers : Wond'rous men,
Ye, whose skill'd fingers know how best to lead
Thro' all the maze of sound, the wayward step
Of Harmony, guiding her varied course
Thro' dissonance to concord, sweetest then
Ev'n when expected harshest. MADOR, thou
Full oft shalt interpose : Thy spirit sublime
Can burst in unpremeditated strains
Of Poesy, that scorn the warbling aid
Of voice or harp. Thou hast the key, great Bard!
That best can ope the portal of the soul ;
Unlock it straight, and lead the pensive Pilgrim
Through the vast regions of futurity.

O D E.

A I R.

Second B A R D.

Hail! thou harp of Phrygian frame!
  In years of yore that Camber bore
From Troy's sepulchral flame ;
  With ancient BRUTE, to Britain's shore
The mighty minstrel came :

R E C I T A T I V E accompanied.

Fourth B A R D.

  Sublime upon thy burnish'd prow,
  He bad thy manly modes to flow ;

A I R.

Britain heard the descant bold,
  She flung her white arms o'er the sea ;
Proud in her leafy bosom to enfold
  The freight of harmony.

M A D O R.

Mute 'till then was ev'ry plain,
  Save where the flood o'er mountains rude
Tumbled his tide amain :
  And Echo from th' impending wood
Resounded the hoarse strain ;

D   While

While from the north the fullen gale
With hollow whiftlings fhook the vale;
Difmal notes, and anfwer'd foon
  By favage howl the heaths among,
What time the wolf doth bay the trembling moon,
  And thin the bleating throng.
  Thou fpak'ft, imperial Lyre,
The rough roar ceas'd, and airs from high
Lapt the land in extafy:
  Fancy, the fairy with thee came;
  And Infpiration, bright-ey'd dame,
Oft at thy call would leave her fapphire fky;
  And, if not vain the verfe prefumes,
Ev'n now fome chafte Divinity is near:
  For lo! the found of diftant plumes
Pants thro' the pathlefs defart of the air.
  'Tis not the flight of her;
  'Tis Sleep, her dewy harbinger.

Second B A R D.

Change my harp, Oh change thy meafures;
Cull, from thy mellifluous treafures,
  Notes that fteal on even feet,
Ever flow, yet never paufing,
  Mixt with many a warble fweet,
In a ling'ring cadence clofing.

M A D O R.

Now the pleas'd pow'r finks gently down the fkies,
And feals with hand of down the Druid's flumb'ring eyes.
Thrice I paufe, and thrice I found   [*Symphony.*
  The central ftring, and now I ring
(By meafur'd lore profound)   [*Symphony.*
  A fevenfold chime, and fweep, and fwing,
Above, below, around,
  To mix thy mufic with the fpheres,
  That warble to immortal ears.   [*Symphony.*
                                                    In-

Infpiration hears the call;
   She rifes from her throne above,
And, fudden as the glancing meteors fall,
   She comes, fhe fills the grove.
High her port; her waving hand
   A pencil bears; the days, the years,
Arife at her command,
   And each obedient colouring wears.
Lo, where Time's pictur'd band
   In hues ethereal glide along;
   Oh mark the tranfitory throng;
Now they dazzle, now they die,
   Inftant they flit from light to fhade,
Mark the blue forms of faint futurity,
   Oh mark them ere they fade.
   Whence was that inward groan?
Why burfts thro' clofed lids the tear?
Why uplifts the briftling hair
   Its white and venerable fhade?
   Why down the confecrated head
Courfes in chilly drops the dew of fear?
   All is not well, the pale-ey'd moon
Curtains her head in clouds, the ftars retire,
   Save from the fultry fouth alone
The fwart ftar flings his peftilential fire;
   Ev'n Sleep herfelf will fly,
   If not recall'd by Harmony.

         Third B A R D.

Wake, my lyre! thy foftest numbers,
Such as nurfe ecftatic flumbers,
Sweet as tranquil Virtue feels
   When the toil of life is ending,
While from the earth the fpirit fteals,
   And, on new-born plumes afcending,

           Haftens

Haſtens to lave in the bright fount of day,
'Till Deſtiny prepare a ſhrine of purer clay.

M O D R E D, *waking, ſpeaks.*

It may not be. Avaunt terrific axe;
Why hangs thy bright edge glaring o'er the grove?
Oh for a giant's nerve to ward the ſtroke!
It bows, it falls.
Where am I? huſh, my ſoul!
'Twas all a dream. Reſume no more the ſtrain:
The midnight air falls chilly on my breaſt;
And now I ſhiver, now a fev'riſh glow
Scorches my vitals. Hark! ſome ſtep approaches.

S C E N E V.

E V E L I N A, M O D R E D, C H O R U S.

E V E L I N A.

Thus, with my wayward fears, to burſt unbidden
On your dread ſynod, rouſing, as ye ſeem,
From holy trance, appears a deſperate deed,
Ev'n to the wretch who dares it.

M O D R E D.

Virgin! quickly
Pronounce the cauſe.

E V E L I N A.

Bear with a ſimple maid
Too prone to fear, perchance my fears are vain.

M O D R E D.

But yet declare them.

E V E L I N A.

I ſuſpect me much
The faith of theſe Brigantes.

M O D R E D.

Say'ſt thou, Virgin?
Heed what thou ſay'ſt; Suſpicion is a gueſt

That

That in the breaft of man, of wrathful man,
Too oft' his welcome finds; yet feldom fure ·
In that fubmiffive calm that fmooths the mind
Of maiden innocence.

EVELINA.

I know it well:
Yet muft I ftill diftruft the elder ftranger:
For while he talks, (and much the flatterer talks)
His brother's filent carriage gives difproof
Of all his wordy boaft. Oft too I faw
A figh unbidden heave the younger's breaft,
Half check'd as it was rais'd; fometimes, methought,
His gentle eye would caft a glance on me,
As if he pitied me; and then again
Would faften on my father, gazing there
To veneration; then he'd figh again,
Look on the ground, and hang his modeft head
Moft penfively.

MODRED.

This may demand, my brethren,
More ferious fearch: Virgin! proceed.

EVELINA.

'Tis true,
My father, rapt in high heroic zeal,
Heeds not the diff'rent carriage of thefe brethren.
Yet fure 'tis ftrange, if, as the tale reports,
My mother fojourns with this diftant Queen,
She fhould not fend or to my fire, or me,
Some fond remembrance of her love? ah! none,
With tears I fpeak it, none, not her dear bleffing
Has reach'd my longing ears.

MODRED.

The Gods, my brethren,
Infpire thefe fcruples; oft to female foftnefs,
Oft to the purity of virgin fouls,
Doth Heav'n its voluntary light difpenfe,

When

When victims bleed in vain. They muft be fpies.
Hie thee, good CANTABER, and to our prefence
Summon the young Brigantian.

EVELINA.

Do not that,
Or, if ye do, yet treat him nothing fternly:
The fofteft terms from fuch a tender breaft
Will draw confeffion, and, if ye fhall find
The treafon ye fufpect, forbear to curfe him.
(Not that my weaknefs means to guide your wifdom)
Yet, as I think he would not wittingly
E'er do a deed of bafenefs, were it granted
That I might queftion him, my heart forebodes
It more could gain by gentlenefs and prayers,
Than will the fierceft threats.

MODRED.

Perchance it may:
And quickly fhalt thou try. But fee the King!
And with him both the youths.

EVELINA.

Alas! my fears
Forewent my errand, elfe had I inform'd thee
That therefore did I come, and from my father
To gain admiffion. Mark the younger, Druid,
How fad he feems; oft did he in the cave
So fold his arms——

MODRED.

We mark him much, and much
The elder's free and dreadlefs confidence.
Virgin, retire awhile in yonder vale,
Nor, 'till thy royal fa her quits the grove,
Refume thy ftation here.   [*Exit Evelina.*

SCENE

S C E N E VI.

CARACTACUS, MODRED, VELLINUS, ELI-
DURUS, CHORUS.

C A R A C T A C U S.

Forgive me, Druid!
My eager foul no longer could fuftain
The pangs of expectation; the great caufe,
I truft, abfolves me: Fathers, it is yours;
'Tis freedom's, 'tis the caufe of Heav'n itfelf;
And fure Heav'n owns it fuch.

M O D R E D.

CARACTACUS,
All that by fage and fanctimonious rites
Might of the Gods be afk'd, we have effay'd;
And yet, nor to our wifh, nor to their wont,
Gave they benign affent.

C A R A C T A C U S.

Death to our hopes!

M O D R E D.

While yet we lay in facred flumber tranc'd,
Sullen and fad to Fancy's frighted eye
Did fhapes of dun and murky hue advance,
In train tumultuous; ftarting we awoke,
Yet felt no waking calm; ftill all was dark:
Sufpicious tremors ftill————

V E L L I N U S.

Of what fufpicious?
Druid, our Queen————

M O D R E D.

Reftrain thy wayward tongue,
Infolent youth! in fuch licentious mood
To interrupt our fpeech ill fuits thy years,
And worfe our fanctity.

CARAC-

CARACTACUS.
'Tis his diftrefs
Makes him forget, what elfe his reverent zeal
Would pay ye holily. Think what he feels,
Poor youth! who fears yon moon, before fhe wanes;
May fee his country conquer'd; fee his Mother,
The victor's flave, her royal blood debas'd,
Dragging her chains thro' the throng'd ftreets of Rome,
To grace oppreffion's triumph.

VELLINUS.
Monarch, yes;
If Heav'n reftrains thy formidable fword,
Or to its ftroke denies that juft fuccefs
Which Heav'n alone can give, I fear me much
Our Queen, ourfelves, nay Britain's felf, muft perifh.

CARACTACUS.
But is not this a fear makes Virtue vain?
Tears from yon miniftring regents of the fky
Their right? Plucks from firm-handed Providence,
The golden reins of fublunary fway;
And gives them to blind Chance? Nay, frown not, Druid,
I do not think 'tis thus.

MODRED.
We truft thou do'ft not.

CARACTACUS.
Mafters of Wifdom! No: my foul confides
In that all-healing and all-forming Power,
Who, on the radiant day when Time was born,
Caft his broad eye upon the wild of ocean,
And calm'd it with a glance: then, plunging deep
His mighty arm, pluck'd from its dark domain
This throne of Freedom, lifted it to light,
Girt it with filver cliffs, and call'd it Britain:
He did, and will preferve it.

MODRED.

M O D R E D.

Pious Prince !
In that all-healing and all-forming power
Still let thy foul confide; but not in men,
No, not in thefe, ingenuous as they feem,
'Till they are try'd by that high teft of faith
Our ancient laws ordain.

V E L L I N U S.

Illuftrious Seer !
Methinks our Sov'reign's fignet well might plead
Her envoy's faith. Thy pardon, mighty Druid,
Not for ourfelves, but for our Queen we plead;
Miftrufting us, ye wound her honour.

M O D R E D.

Peace;
Our will admits no parley. Thither, Youths,
Turn your aftonifh'd eyes; behold yon huge
And unhewn fphere of living adamant,
Which, pois'd by magic, refts its central weight
On yonder pointed rock : firm as it feems,
Such is its ftrange and virtuous property,
It moves obfequious to the gentleft touch
Of him, whofe breaft is pure; but to a traitor,
Tho' ev'n a giant's prowefs nerv'd his arm,
It ftands as fixt as Snowdon. No reply;
The Gods command that one of you muft now
Approach and try it: in your fnowy vefts,
Ye Priefts, involve the lots, and to the younger,
As is our wont, tender the choice of Fate.

E L I D U R U S.

Heav'ns ! is it fall'n on me ?

M O D R E D.

Young Prince, it is;
Prepare thee for thy trial.

E L I D U R U S.

Gracious Gods !

E   Who

Who may look up to your tremendous thrones,
And fay his breaſt is pure? All-ſearching Pow'rs,
Ye know already how and what I am;
And what ye mean to publiſh me in Mona,
To that I yield and tremble.

CARACTACUS.

Rouſe thee, Youth!
And, with that courage honeſt Truth ſupplies,
(For ſure ye both are true) haſte to the trial;
Behold I lead thee on.

MODRED.

Prince, we arreſt
Thy haſty ſtep: Know, e'er he meet that trial,
He muſt be plung'd into the dark drear womb
Of this deep cavern, which the yawning Earth,
Struck with our wand, now opens to thy view.
A thouſand rugged ſteps of moſs-grown rock
Lead to its horrible baſe. Low as that baſe,
Where never ray of chearing light yet ſhot,
The youth muſt now deſcend; there ſhall he ſit,
With ſolitude and ſilence compaſs'd round,
Till our recalling clarion bids him climb
Again to our dread preſence. Meanwhile there,
Ev'n in the centre of that perilous pit,
The ſolemn recollection of his deeds
Done, or deſign'd, ſhall paſs in cold review
Before him; horror then ſhall ſhake his ſoul,
If, in the varied file, one deed be found
Alien to Truth and Virtue.   [*Elidurus deſcends.*

To thy charge,
CARACTACUS, his brother we conſign.
Guard him in yonder cave. The trial paſt,
Again will we confer, touching that part
Which Heav'n's high will ordains thee to perform.

END *of the* SECOND ACT.

ACT

A C T III.

S C E N E I.

The curtain draws up, while a flow march is played.
MODRED, &c. *open the cavern in which* ELIDURUS
was confined: they lead him in procession round the al-
tar, and from thence to the rocking stone: then the
following Ode is performed by MADOR *and the Bards.*

O D E.

R E C I T A T I V E *accompanied.*
Second B A R D.

*T*HOU *Spirit pure, that spread'st unseen*
 Thy pinions o'er this pond'rous sphere,
And, breathing thro' each rigid vein,
Fill'st with stupendous life the marble mass,
And bid'st it bow upon its base,
 When sov'reign Truth is near;
Full C H O R U S.

Spirit invisible! to thee
We swell the solemn harmony.

A I R and C H O R U S.

 Hear us, and aid:
Thou that in Virtue's cause
O'er-rulest Nature's laws,
Oh hear, and aid with influence high
The sons of Peace and Piety.

M A D O R,

 First-born of that ethereal tribe
Call'd into birth ere time or place,
 Whom wave nor wind can circumscribe,
Heirs of the liquid liberty of Light,
That float on rainbow pennons bright
 Thro' all the wilds of space,
Yet thou alone of all thy kind
Can'st range the regions of the mind,

E 2

Thou

Thou only know'ft
That dark meandring maze,
Where wayward Falfehood ftrays,
And, feizing fwift the lurking fprite,
Forceft her forth to fhame and light.
Thou can'ft enter the dark cell
Where the vulture Confcience flumbers,
And, unarm'd by charming fpell,
Or magic numbers,
Can'ft roufe her from her formidable fleep,
And bid her dart her raging talons deep;
Yet, ah! too feldom doth the furious fiend
Thy bidding wait; vindictive, felf-prepar'd,
She knows her torturing time; too fure to rend
The trembling heart, when Virtue quits her guard.
Paufe then, celeftial gueft!
And, brooding on thine adamantine fphere,
If fraud approach, Spirit, that fraud declare:
To Confcience and to Mona leave the reft.

RECITATIVE accompanied.
Fourth BARD.

Paufe then, celeftial gueft!
And, brooding on thine adamantine fphere,
If fraud approach, Spirit, that fraud declare:
To Confcience and to Mona leave the reft.

Full CHORUS.

To Confcience and to Mona leave the reft.

MODRED.

Heard'ft thou the awful invocation, Youth,
Wrapt in thofe holy harpings?

ELIDURUS.

Sage, I did;
And it came o'er my foul as doth the thunder,
While diftant yet, with an expected burft,
It threats the trembling ear. Now to the trial.

MODRED.

Ere that, bethink thee well what rig'rous doom

Attends

Attends thine act: if failing, certain death.
So certain, that in our abfolving tongues
Refts not that power may fave thee : thou muft die.

S C E N E II.

EVELINA, ELIDURUS, MODRED, CHORUS.

E V E L I N A.

Die, fay'ft thou ? Druid !

E L I D U R U S.

Evelina here !

Lead to the rock.

M O D R E D.

No, youth, awhile we fpare thee ;
And, in our ftead, permit this royal maiden
To urge thee firft with virgin gentlenefs.
Refpect our clemency, and meet her queftions
With anfwers prompt and true: fo may'ft thou 'fcape
A fterner trial.

E L I D U R U S.

Rather to the rock.——

E V E L I N A.

Doft thou difdain me, Prince ? Loft as I am,
Methinks the daughter of CARACTACUS
Might merit milder treatment : I was born
To royal hopes and promife, nurs'd i' th' lap
Of foft Profperity ; alas the change !
I meant but to addrefs a few brief words
To this young Prince, and he doth turn his eye,
And fcorns to anfwer me.

E L I D U R U S.

Scorn thee ! fweet maid ?

No ; 'tis the fear——

E V E L I N A.

And can'ft thou fear me, Youth ?
Ev'n while I led a life of royalty,
I bore myfelf to all with meek deportment,

In

In nothing harſh, or cruel: and, howe'er
Misfortune works upon the minds of men,
(For ſome, they ſay, it turns to very ſtone)
Mine, I am ſure, it ſoftens. Wert thou guilty,
Yet I ſhould pity thee; nay, wert thou leagued
To load this ſuffering heart with more misfortuncs,
Still ſhould I pity thee; nor e'er believe
Thou would'ſt, on free and voluntary choice,
Betray the innocent.

ELIDURUS.

Indeed I would not.

EVELINA.

No, gracious Youth, I do believe thou would'ſt not;
For on thy brow the liberal hand of Heav'n
Has portray'd Truth as viſible and bold,
As were the pictur'd ſuns that deckt the brows
Of our brave anceſtors. Say then, young Prince,
(For therefore have I wiſh'd to queſtion thee)
Bring ye no token of a mother's fondneſs
To her expecting child? A captive Queen
Has more than common claim for pity, Prince!
And ev'n the ills of venerable age
Were cauſe enough to move thy tender nature.
The tears o'ercharge thine eye. Alas, my fears!
Sickneſs or ſore infirmity had ſeiz'd her
Before thou left'ſt the palace, elſe her lips
Had to thy care entruſted ſome kind meſſage,
And bleſt her hapleſs daughter by thy tongue.
Would ſhe were here!

ELIDURUS.

Would Heav'n ſhe were!

EVELINA.

Ah, why?

ELIDURUS.

Becauſe you wiſh it.

EVE-

EVELINA.

Thanks, ingenuous Youth,
For this thy courtefy. Yet, if the Queen
Thy mother fhines with fuch rare qualities,
As late thy brother boafted, fhe will calm
Her woes, and I fhall clafp her aged knees
Again in peace and liberty.———Alas!
He fpeaks not; all my fears are juft.

ELIDURUS.

What fears?

The Queen GUIDERIA is not dead.

EVELINA.

Not dead!

But is fhe in that happy ftate of freedom
Which we were taught to hope? Why figh'ft thou, Youth?
Thy years have yet been profp'rous. Did thy father
E'er lofe a kingdom? Did captivity
E'er feize thy fhrieking mother? Thou can'ft go
To yonder cave, and find thy brother fafe:
He is not loft as mine is. Youth, thou figh'ft
Again; thou haft not fure fuch caufe for forrow;
But if thou haft, give me thy griefs, I pray thee;
I have a heart can foftly fympathize,
And fympathy is foothing.

ELIDURUS.

O Gods! Gods!

She tears my foul. What fhall I fay?

EVELINA.

Perchance,

For all in this bad world muft have their forrows,
Thou too haft thine; and may'ft, like me, be wretched.
Haply amid the woes thefe fons of blood
Bring on our groaning country, fome chafte maid,
Whofe tender foul was link'd by love to thine,
Might fall the trembling prey to Roman rage,
Ev'n at the golden hour when holy rites

Had

Had feal'd your virtuous vows. If it were fo,
Indeed I pity her!

E L I D U R U S.

Not that: not that.
Never till now did beauty's matchlefs beam——
But I am dumb.

E V E L I N A.

Why that dejected eye?
And why this filence? That fome weighty grief
O'erhangs thy foul, thy ev'ry look proclaims.
Why then refufe it words? The heart that bleeds
From any ftroke of fate or human wrongs,
Loves to difclofe itfelf, that lift'ning Pity
May drop a healing tear upon the wound.
'Tis only, when with inbred horror fmote
At fome bafe act, or done, or to be done,
That the recoiling foul, with confcious dread,
Shrinks back into itfelf. But thou, good Youth—

E L I D U R U S.

Ceafe, royal maid! permit me to depart.—

E V E L I N A.

Yet hear me, ftranger! Truth and Secrefy,
Tho' friends, are feldom neceffary friends—

E L I D U R U S.

I go to try my truth.—

E V E L I N A.

O! go not hence
In wrath; think not that I fufpect thy virtue:
Yet ignorance may oft make virtue flide,
And if——

E L I D U R U S.

In pity fpare me.

E V E L I N A.

If thy brother——
Nay, ftart not, do not turn thine eye from mine;
Speak, I conjure thee, is his purpofe honeft?

I know the guilty price that barb'rous Rome
Sets on my Father's head; and gold, vile gold,
Has now a charm for Britons :—Yes, thou fhudder'ft
At the dire thought; yet not as if 'twere ftrange,
But as our fears were mutual. Ah! young ftranger,
That open face fcarce needs a tongue to utter
What works within. Come then, ingenuous Prince,
And inftant make difcovery to the Druid,
While yet 'tis not too late.

E L I D U R U S.

Ah! what difcover?
Say, whom muft I betray?

E V E L I N A.

Thy brother.

E L I D U R U S.

Ha!

E V E L I N A.

Who is no brother, if his guilty foul
Teems with fuch perfidy. O all ye ftars!
Can he be brother to a youth like thee,
Who would betray an old and honour'd King,
That King his countryman, the pride of Britain?
Can he be brother to a youth like thee,
Who from a young, defencelefs, innocent maid,
Would take that King her father? Make her fuffer
All that an orphan fuffers? More perchance:
The ruffian foe.—O tears, ye choak my utterance!
It cannot be——and yet thou ftill art filent.
Turn, Youth, and fee me weep: ah, fee me kneel.
I am of royal blood, not wont to kneel,
Yet will I kneel to thee. Oh fave my father!
Save a diftrefsful maiden from the force
Of barbarous men! Be thou a brother to me,
For mine, alas!——Ha!

[Sees *Arviragus entering.*

F   S C E N E

SCENE III.

ARVIRAGUS, EVELINA, ELIDURUS,
MODRED, CHORUS.

ARVIRAGUS.

Evelina, rife!
Know, maid, I ne'er will tamely fee thee kneel,
Ev'n at the foot of Cæsar.

EVELINA.

'Tis himfelf:
And he will prove my father's fears were falfe;
Falfe, as his fon is brave. Thou beft of brothers,
Come to my arms. Where haft thou been, thou wanderer?
How wert thou fav'd? Indeed, Arviragus,
I never fhed fuch tears, fince thou wert loft,
For thefe are tears of rapture.

ARVIRAGUS.

Evelina!
Fain wou'd I greet thee as a brother ought:
But wherefore did'ft thou kneel?

EVELINA.

Oh! afk not now.

ARVIRAGUS.

By heav'n I muft; and he muft anfwer me,
Whoe'er he be. What art thou, fullen ftranger?

ELIDURUS.

A Briton.

ARVIRAGUS.

Brief and bold.

EVELINA.

Ah, fpare the taunt:
He merits not thy wrath. Behold the Druids:
Lo! they advance. With holy reverence firft
Thou muft addrefs their fanctity.

ARVI-

A R V I R A G U S.

I will.
But fee, proud Boy, thou do'ft not quit the grove
'Till time allows us parley.

E L I D U R U S.

Prince, I mean not.
[*Elidurus retires among the Chorus.*

A R V I R A G U S.

Sages, and fons of heav'n! Illuftrious Druids!
Abruptly I approach your facred prefence:
Yet fuch dire tidings——

M O D R E D.

On thy peril, peace!
Thou ftand'ft accus'd, and by a father's voice,
Of crimes abhorr'd, of cowardice and flight;
And therefore may'ft not in thefe facred groves
Utter polluted accents. Quickly fay,
Wherefore thou fled'ft? For, that bafe faët unclear'd,
We hold no further converfe.

A R V I R A G U S.

Oh ye Gods!
Am I the fon of your CARACTACUS?
And could I fly?

M O D R E D.

Wafte not or time or words,
But tell us why thou fled'ft.

A R V I R A G U S.

I fled not, Druid!
By the great Gods I fled not! fave to ftop
Our daftard troops, and rally them; when lo!
A random fhaft did level me with earth,
Where, pale and fenfelefs as the flain around me,
I lay till midnight; when a pitying hind
Found me, and fuccour'd me. My ftrength repair'd,
Need I repeat the arts I us'd to fcreen me?
How now a peafant, from a beggarly fcrip

I

I fold cheap food to flaves that nam'd the price,
Nor after gave it.   Now a minftrel poor,
With ill-tun'd harp, I ply'd a thriftlefs trade,
And by fuch fhifts did win obfcurity
To fhroud my name.   At length to other conquefts
OSTORIUS led his legions: fafely now
I to fome valiant friends unmafk'd myfelf,
And with them plann'd how fureft we might draw
Our forces to CAERNARVON.   Here our art
So well avail'd, that now at SNOWDON's foot
Full twenty troops of hardy veterans wait
To call my fire their leader.

M O D R E D.
    Valiant Youth——

E V E L I N A.
He is——I faid he was a valiant Youth;
Nor has he fham'd his race.   Yes, I will fly
And blefs him with the news.

       [Exit Evelina,

S C E N E   IV.

MODRED, ARVIRAGUS, CHORUS.

M O D R E D.
    We do believe
Thy modeft tale: and may the righteous Gods
Thus ever fhed upon thy noble breaft
Difcretion's cooling dew.   When nurtur'd fo,
Then, only then, doth valour bloom mature.

A R V I R A G U S.
Yet vain is valour, howfoe'er it bloom.
Druid, the Gods frown on us.   All my hopes
Are blafted.   I fhall ne'er rejoin my friends;
Ne'er blefs them with my father.   Holy men,
I have a tale to tell, will fhake your fouls.

       Your

Your Mona is invaded: Rome approaches;
Ev'n to these groves approaches.

MODRED.

Horror! horror!

ARVIRAGUS.

Late as I landed on yon higheſt beach,
Where, nodding from the rocks, the poplars fling
Their ſcatter'd arms, and daſh them in the wave;
There were their veſſels moor'd, as if they ſought
Concealment in the ſhade; and as I paſt
Up yon thick-planted ridge, I 'ſpy'd their helms
'Mid brakes and boughs trench'd in the heath below,
Where like a neſt of night-worms did they glitter,
Sprinkling the plain with brightneſs. On I ſped
With ſilent ſtep, yet oft did paſs ſo near,
'Twas next to prodigy I 'ſcap'd unſeen.

MODRED.

Their numbers, Prince?

ARVIRAGUS.

Few, if mine haſty eye
Did find and count them all.

MODRED.

O brethren, brethren!
Treaſon and ſacrilege, worſe foes than Rome,
Have led Rome hither. Inſtant ſeize that wretch,
And bring him to our preſence.

SCENE V.

MODRED, ELIDURUS, ARVIRAGUS, CHORUS.

MODRED.

Say, thou falſe one!
What doom befits the ſlave who ſells his country?

ELIDURUS.

Death, ſudden death!

MO-

M O D R E D.

No; lingering piece-meal death!
And to fuch death thy brother and thyfelf
We now devote. Villain, thy deeds are known!
'Tis known ye led the impious Romans hither
To flaughter us ev'n on our holy altars.

E L I D U R U S.

That on my foul doth lie fome fecret grief
Thefe looks perforce will tell. It is not fear,
Druids, it is not fear that fhakes me thus:
The great Gods know it is not; ye can never:
For, what tho' wifdom lifts ye next thofe gods,
Ye cannot, like to them, unlock men's breafts,
And read their inmoft thoughts. Ah! that ye could.

A R V I R A G U S.

What haft thou done?

E L I D U R U S.

What, Prince, I will not tell.

M O D R E D.

Wretch, there are means——

E L I D U R U S.

I know, and terrible means;
And 'tis both fit that you fhould try thofe means,
And I endure them: yet I think my patience
Will for fome fpace baffle your torturing fury.

M O D R E D.

Be that beft known, when our inflicted goads
Harrow thy flefh!

A R V I R A G U S.

Stranger, ere this is try'd,
Confefs the whole of thy black perfidy:
So black, that when I look upon thy youth,
Read thy mild eye, and mark thy modeft brow,
I think, indeed, thou durft not.

E L I-

ELIDURUS.

Such a crime,
Indeed, I durſt not; and would rather be
The very wretch thou feeſt. I'll ſpeak no more.

MODRED.

Brethren, 'tis ſo. The virgin's thoughts were juſt:
This Youth has been deceiv'd.

ELIDURUS.

Yes, one word more:
You ſay the Romans have invaded Mona.
Give me a ſword and twenty honeſt Britons,
And I will quell thoſe Romans. Vain demand!
Alas! you cannot. Ye are men of peace.
Religion's ſelf forbids. Lead then to torture.

ARVIRAGUS.

Now on my ſoul this Youth doth move me much.

MODRED.

Think not religion and our holy office
Doth teach us tamely, like the bleating lamb,
To crouch before oppreffion, and with neck
Outſtretch'd await the ſtroke. Know, when I blow
That ſacred trumpet bound with ſable fillets
To yonder branching oak, the awful ſound
Calls forth a thouſand Britons train'd alike
In holy and in martial exerciſe;
Not by ſuch mode and rule as Romans uſe,
But of that fierce portentous horrible ſort
As ſhall appall even Romans.

ELIDURUS.

Gracious Gods!
Then there are hopes indeed. Oh call them inſtant:
This Prince will lead them on: I'll follow him,
Tho' in my chains, and ſome way daſh them round
To harm the haughty foe.

ARVI-

ARVIRAGUS.

A thousand Britons!
And arm'd! O instant blow the sacred trump,
And let me head them. Yet methinks this Youth—

MODRED.

I know what thou would'st say: might join thee, Prince?
True; were he free from crime, or had confest.

ELIDURUS.

Confest! ah, think not, I will e'er——

ARVIRAGUS.

Reflect.
Either thyself or brother must have wrong'd us:
Then why conceal——

ELIDURUS.

Hast thou a brother? No!
Else had'st thou spar'd the word; and yet a sister,
Lovely as thine, might more than teach thee, Prince,
What 'tis to have a brother. Hear me, Druids!
Tho' I would prize an hour of freedom now
Before an age of any after date;
Tho' I would seize it as the gift of heav'n,
And use it as heav'n's gift; yet do not think
I so will purchase it. Give it me freely,
I yet will spurn the boon, and hug my chains,
Till you do swear by your own hoary heads,
My brother shall be safe.

MODRED:

Excellent Youth!
Thy words do speak thy soul, and such a soul
As wakes our wonder. Thou art free; thy brother
Shall be thine honour's pledge: so will we use him
As thou art false or true.

ELIDURUS.

I ask no other.

ARVIRAGUS.

Thus then, my fellow soldier, to thy clasp

E

I give the hand of friendſhip. Noble Youth!
We'll ſpeed, or die together.

MODRED.

     Hear us, Prince!
Mona permits not that he fight her battles
'Till duly purified: for tho' his ſoul
Took up unwittingly this deed of baſeneſs,
Yet is luſtration meet. Learn, that in vice
There is a noiſome rankneſs which offends
Heav'n's pure divinities, as us the ſtench
Of pois'nous weed obſcene. Hence doth the man,
Who ev'n converſes with a villain, need
As much purgation as the pallid wretch
'Scap'd from the walls, where frowning Peſtilence
Spreads wide her livid banners. For this cauſe,
Ye Prieſts, conduct the Youth to yonder fount,
And do the needful rites.

      [Exeunt Prieſts with Eiidurus.
     For thee, brave Prince,
Some fit repoſe is needful. To our cave,
Behold, we lead thee; and, ſome moments there
To that repoſe allow'd, we then will bleſs
Thy duteous eyes with their dear father's preſence.

         [Exeunt.

END *of the* THIRD ACT.

-

       ACT

A C T IV.

S C E N E I.

The curtain draws up, and difcovers MODRED *and the* CHORUS *before the altar: then, on one fide, enter* CARACTACUS *and* EVELINA; *on the other,* ARVIRAGUS.

CARACTACUS, ARVIRAGUS, CHORUS, EVELINA.

C A R A C T A C U S.

O My ARVIRAGUS! my fon! my fon!
    What joy, what tranfport, doth thine aged fire
Feel in thefe filial foldings! Speak not, boy,
Nor interrupt that heart-felt ecftacy
Should ftrike us mute. I know what thou would'ft fay,
Yet, prithee, peace. Thy fifter's voice hath clear'd thee,
And, could excufe find words at this bleft moment,
Truft me, I'd give it vent. But 'tis enough;
Thy father welcomes thee to him and honour:
Honour, that now with rapt'rous certainty
Calls thee his own true offspring. Doft thou weep?
Ah, if thy tears fwell not from joy's free fpring,
I beg thee, fpare them. I have done thee wrong;
Can make thee no atonement; none, alas!
Thy father fcarce can blefs thee as he ought;
Unbleft himfelf, befet with foes around,
Bereft of queen, of kingdom, and of foldiers,
He can but give thee portion of his dangers,
Perchance and of his chains: Yet droop not, boy,
Virtue is ftill thine own.

                          ARVI-

ARVIRAGUS.

It is, my Father!
Pure as from thine illuftrious fount it came;
And that unfullied, let the world opprefs us;
Let fraud and falfhood rivet fetters on us;
Still fhall our fouls be free: Yet hope is ours
As well as virtue.

CARACTACUS.

Spoken like a Briton.
True, hope is ours, and therefore let's prepare:
The moments now are precious. Tell us, Druid!
Is it not meet we fee the bands drawn out,
And mark their due array?

MODRED.

Monarch, ev'n now
They fkirt the grove.

CARACTACUS.

Then let us to their front——

MODRED.

But is the traitor-youth in fafety lodg'd?

CARACTACUS.

Druid, he fled——

MODRED.

O fatal flight to Mona!

CARACTACUS.

But what of that? ARVIRAGUS is here;
My fon is here: let then the traitor go.
By this he has join'd the Romans: let him join them;
A fingle arm, and that a villain's arm,
Can lend but little aid to any powers
Oppos'd to truth and virtue. Come, my fon,
Let's to the troops, and marfhal them with fpeed.
That done, we from thefe venerable men
Will claim their ready bleffing: then to battle;

And

And the fwift fun, ev'n at his purple dawn,
Shall fpy us crown'd with conqueft, or with death.

[*Exeunt Caraĉtacus and Arviragus.*

S C E N E II.

MODRED, EVELINA, CHORUS.

MODRED.

What may his flight portend? Say, EVELINA!
How came this youth to 'fcape?

EVELINA.

And that to tell
Will fix much blame on my impatient folly:
For, ere your hallow'd lips had given permiffion,
I flew with eager hafte to bear my father
News of his fon's return. But my rafh tongue
Scarce nam'd ARVIRAGUS, ere the falfe ftranger
Fled to the cavern's mouth.

MODRED.

The king purfued?

EVELINA.

Alas! he mark'd him not, for 'twas the moment
When he had all to afk, and all to fear,
Touching my brother's valour: yet he foon
Perceiv'd his prifoner gone, and with fierce glance
Survey'd the cavern round; then fnatch'd his fpear,
And menac'd to purfue the flying traitor:
But I with prayers (O pardon if they err'd!)
Withheld his ftep, for to the left the youth
Had wing'd his way, where the thick underwood
Afforded fure retreat.

MODRED.

Maiden, enough.
Better, perchance, for us, if he were captive:
But in the juftice of their caufe, and heav'n,
Do Mona's fons confide.

SCENE

S C E N E III.

BARD, MODRED, ELIDURUS, EVELINA, CHORUS.

B A R D.

        · Druid, the rites
Are finifh'd ; all fave that which crowns the reft,
And which pertains to thy bleft hand alone :
For that he kneels before thee.

M O D R E D.

        Take him hence :
We may not truft him forth to fight our caufe.

E L I D U R U S,

Now by ANDRASTE's throne——

M O D R E D.

        Nay, fwear not, Youth ;
The tie is broke that held thy fealty :
Thy brother's fled.

E L I D U R U S.

        Fled !

M O D R E D.

        To the Romans fled.
Yes ; thou haft caufe to tremble.

E L I D U R U S.

        Ah, VELLINUS !
Does thus our love, does thus our friendfhip end ?
Was I thy brother, youth, and haft thou left me ?
Yes ; and how left me ? cruel as thou art,
The victim of thy crimes !

M O D R E D.

        True : thou muft die.

E L I D U R U S.

I pray ye then on your beft mercy, Fathers,
It may be fpeedy. I would fain be dead,
If this be life : yet I muft doubt ev'n that ;

                      For

For falfhood of this ftrange ftupendous fort
Sets firm-ey'd Reafon on a gaze, miftrufting
That what fhe fees in palpable plain form,
The ftars in yon blue arch, thefe woods, thefe caverns,
Are all meer tricks of cozenage; nothing real;
The vifion of a vifion. If he's fled,
I ought to hate this brother.

M O D R E D.

Yet thou doft not,

E L I D U R U S.

But when aftonifhment will give me leave,
Perchance I fhall.—And yet he is my brother;
And he was virtuous once. Yes, ye vile Romans!
Yes, I muft die before my thirfty fword
Drinks one rich drop of vengeance. Yet, ye robbers!
Yet will I curfe you with my dying lips:
'Twas you that ftole away my brother's virtue.

M O D R E D.

Now then prepare to die.

E L I D U R U S.

I am prepar'd.
Yet, fince I cannot now (what moft I wifh'd)
By manly prowefs guard this lovely maid,
Permit that on your holieft earth I kneel,
And pour one fervent prayer for her protection.
Allow me this; for, though you think me falfe,
The Gods will hear me.

E V E L I N A.

I can hold no longer.
O Druid, Druid, at thy feet I fall!
Yes, I muft plead, (away with virgin-blufhes)
For fuch a youth muft plead. I'll die to fave him.
O take my life, and let him fight for Mona.

M O D R E D.

Virgin, arife. His virtue hath redeem'd him,
And he fhall fight for thee, and for his country.

Youth,

Youth, thank us with thy deeds. The time is fhort,
And now with reverence take our high luftration:
Thrice do we fprinkle thee with day-break dew
Shook from the May-thorn bloffom; twice and thrice
Touch we thy forehead with our holy wand:
Now thou art fully purg'd. Now rife reftor'd
To virtue and to us. Hence then, my fon,
Hie thee to yonder altar, where our Bards
Shall arm thee duly both with helm and fword
For warlike enterprize. *Exit Elidurus.*

S C E N E   IV.

CARACTACUS, ARVIRAGUS, EVELINA, MODRED, CHORUS.

C A R A C T A C U S.
'Tis true, my Son!
Bold are their bearings, and I fear me not
But they have hearts will not belie their looks.
I like them well. Yet would to righteous heav'n
Thofe valiant veterans that on Snowdon guard
Their fcanty pittance of bleak liberty
Were here to join them; we would teach thefe wolves,
Tho' we permit their rage to prowl our coafts,
That vengeance waits them ere they rob our altars.
Hail, Druid, hail! we find thy valiant guards
Accoutred fo, as well befpeaks the wifdom
That fram'd their phalanx. We but wait thy blefling
To lead them 'gainft the foe.
M O D R E D.
CARACTACUS!
Behold this fword: The fword of old BELINUS,
Stain'd with the blood of giants, and its name
TRIFINGUS. Many an age its charmed blade
Has flept within yon confecrated trunk.
Lo, I unfheath it, King! upon thy knee

Receive

Receive the facred pledge. And, mark our words—
By the bright circle of the golden fun;
By the brief courfes of the errant moon;
By the dread potency of every ftar
That ftuds the myftic zodiac's burning girth;
By each, and all of thefe fupernal figns,
We do adjure thee with this trufty blade,
To guard yon central Oak, whofe holieft ftem
Involves the fpirit of high TARANIS:
This be thy charge; to which in aid we join
Ourfelves, and our fage brethren. With our vaffals
Thy Son and the Brigantian Prince fhall make
Incurfion on the foe.

CARACTACUS.

                    In this, and all,
Be ours obfervance meet. Yet furely, Druid,
The frefh and active vigour of thefe youths
Might better fuit with this important charge.
Not that my heart fhrinks at the glorious tafk,
But will with ready zeal pour forth its blood
Upon the facred roots, my firmeft courage
Might fail to fave. Yet, Fathers, I am old;
And if I fell the foremoft in the onfet,
Should leave a fon behind, might ftill defend you.

MODRED.

The facred adjuration we have utter'd
May never be recall'd.

CARACTACUS.

                    Then be it fo.
But do not think I counfel this thro' fear:
Old as I am, I truft with half our powers
I could drive back thefe Romans to their fhips;
Daftards, that come as doth the cow'ring fowler
To tangle me with fnares and take me tamely:
Slaves, they fhall find, that ere they gain their prey,
They have to hunt it boldly with barb'd fpears,

                                        And

And meet such conflict as the chafed boar
Gives to his stout assailants.   O ye Gods!
That I might instant face them.

M O D R E D.

Be thy Son's
The onset.

A R V I R A G U S.

From his soul that son doth thank ye,
Blessing the wisdom that preserves his father
Thus to the last.   Steel then, ye powers of Heav'n!
Steel my firm soul with your own fortitude,
Free from alloy of passion.   Give me courage,
That knows not rage; revenge, that knows not malice;
Let me not thirst for carnage, but for conquest:
And conquest gain'd, sleep vengeance in my breast,
Ere in its sheath my sword.

C A R A C T A C U S.

Oh hear his Father!
If ever rashness spurr'd me on, great Gods,
To acts of danger thirsting for renown;
If e'er my eager soul pursu'd its course
Beyond just Reason's limit, visit not
My faults on him.   I am the thing you made me,
Vindictive, bold, precipitate, and fierce:
But as you gave to him a milder mind,
O bless him, bless him with a milder fate!

E V E L I N A.

Nor yet unheard let EVELINA pour
Her pray'rs and tears.   Oh hear a hapless maid,
That ev'n thro' half the years her life has number'd,
Ev'n nine long years has dragg'd a trembling being,
Beset with pains and perils.   Give her peace;
And, to endear it more, be that blest peace
Won by her brother's sword.   Oh bless his arm,
And bless his valiant followers, One,—and all.

E L I-

ELIDURUS *entering armed:*

Hear, Heav'n! and let this pure and virgin prayer
Plead ev'n for ELIDURUS, whose sad soul
Cannot look up to your immortal thrones,
And urge his own request: Else would he ask,
That all the dangers of th' approaching fight
Might fall on him alone: That every spear
The Romans wield might at his breast be aim'd;
Each arrow darted on his rattling helm;
That so the brother of this beauteous maid,
Returning safe with victory and peace,
Might bear them to her bosom.

MODRED.
                              Now rise all,
And Heav'n, that knows, what most ye ought to ask,
Grant all ye ought to have.   Behold, the stars
Are faded; universal darkness reigns.
Now is the dreadful hour, now will our torches
Glare with more livid horror, now our shrieks,
And clanking arms will more appall the foe.
But heed, ye Bards, that for the sign of onset,
Ye found the antientest of all your rhymes,
Whose birth tradition notes not, nor who fram'd
Its lofty strains: The force of that high air
Did JULIUS feel, when, fir'd by it, our fathers
First drove the robber recreant to his ships.
Now forth, brave Pair! Go, with our blessing go;
Mute be the march, as ye ascend the hill:
Then, when ye hear the sound of our shrill trumpet,
Fall on the foe.

CARACTACUS.
                    And glory be thy guide;
Pride of my soul, go forth and conquer.

EVELINA.
                              Brother,
Yet one embrace.   O thou much-honour'd Stranger,

I

I charge thee fight by my dear brother's fide,
And fhield him from the foe; for he is brave,
And will, with bold and well-directed arm,
Return thy fuccour. [*Exeunt Arviragus and Elidurus.*

M O D R E D.

           Now, ye Priefts, with fpeed
Strew on the altar's height your facred leaves,
And light the morning flame. But why is this?
Why doth our brother MADOR fnatch his harp
From yonder bough? Why this way bend his ftep?

C A R A C T A C U S.

He is entranc'd. The fillet burfts that bound
His liberal locks; his fnowy veftments fall
In ampler folds; and all his floating form
Doth feem to gliften with divinity!
Yet is he fpeechlefs. Say, thou Chief of Bards,
What is there in this airy vacancy,
That thou with fiery and irregular glance
Should'ft fcan thus wildly? wherefore heaves thy breaft?
Why ftarts——

O D E.

M A D O R.

Hark!   [*Symphony behind the Scenes.*
    Hark!   [*Symphony louder.*
        Hark!   [*Full Symphony.*
Hark! heard ye not yon footftep dread,
That fhook the earth with thund'ring tread?
   'Twas Death.—In hafte
   The Warrior paft;
High tower'd his helmed head:
  I mark'd his mail, I mark'd his fhield,
I 'fpy'd the fparkling of his fpear,
  I faw his giant arm the falchion wield;
Wide wav'd the bick'ring blade, and fir'd the angry air.

On me (he cry'd) my Britons, wait,
To lead you to the field of fate
   · I come : Yon car,
    That cleaves the air,
Defcends to throne my ftate :
   I mount your Champion and your God.
My proud fteeds neigh beneath the thong :
   Hark ! to my wheels of brafs, that rattle loud !
Hark ! to my clarion fhrill, that brays the woods among !
Full C H O R U S.

He mounts our Champion and our God.
His proud fteeds neigh beneath the thong :
   Hark ! to his wheels of brafs, that rattle loud !
Hark ! to his clarion fhrill, that brays the woods among !
M A D O R.

Fear not now the Fever's fire,
   Fear not now the Death-bed groan,
Pangs that torture, pains that tire,
   Bed-rid age with feeble moan :
Thefe domeftic terrors wait
Hourly at my palace gate ;
   And when o'er flothful realms my rod I wave,
   Thefe on the tyrant King and coward Slave,
Rufh with vindictive rage, and drag them to their grave.

But ye, my Sons, at this high hour
Shall fhare the fullnefs of my pow'r :
   From all your bows,
   In level'd rows,
My own dread fhafts fhall fhower.
   Go then to conqueft, gladly go,
Deal forth my dole of deftiny,
   With all my fury dafh the trembling foe
Down to thofe darkfome dens, where Rome's pale
      fpectres lie ;

Where

Where creeps the ninefold ſtream profound
Her black inexorable round,
 And on the bank,
 To willows dank,
The ſhivering ghoſts are bound.
 Twelve thouſand creſcents all ſhall ſwell
To full-orb'd pride, and fading die,
 Ere they again in life's gay manſions dwell:
Not ſuch the meed that crowns the ſons of Liberty.

No, my Britons! battle-ſlain,
 Rapture gilds your parting hour:
I, that all deſpotic reign,
 Claim but there a moment's power.
Swiftly the ſoul of Britiſh flame
Animates ſome kindred frame,
 Swiftly to life and light triumphant flies,
 Exults again in martial ecſtacies,
Again for freedom fights, again for freedom dies.
  Full C H O R U S.
The godlike ſoul of Britiſh flame
Animates ſome kindred frame,
 Swiftly to life and light triumphant flies,
 Exults again in martial ecſtacies,
Again for freedom fights, again for freedom dies.

         [Exeunt.

END *of the* FOURTH ACT.

        A C T

E

A C T V.

S C E N E I.

Enter CARACTACUS *haftily, but with-held by* MODRED *and the* CHORUS.

C A R A C T A C U S.

DRUID, with-hold me not. The thundering voice
  Still rolls around my ear. Death calls to arms,
Hark! Hark! he calls again! Champion, lead on,
I follow; give me way, my foul is Britifh;
Does he not fay unconquered, undifmay'd,
The Britifh foul revives? Yes, fome bleft fhaft
Shall rid me of this clog of cumb'rous age;
And I again fhall in fome happier mould
Rife to redeem my country.

M O D R E D.

                         Stay thee, Prince,
And mark what clear and amber-fkirted clouds
Rife from the altar's verge, and cleave the fkies:
Oh 'tis a profperous omen! Soon expect
To hear glad tidings.

C A R A C T A C U S.

                        I will fend them to thee.

M O D R E D.

But fee, a Bard approaches, and he bears them:
Elfe is his eye no herald to his heart.

S C E N E II.

BARD, MODRED, CARACTACUS, CHORUS.

C A R A C T A C U S.

Speedily tell thy tale.

B A R D.

                   A tale like mine,

I truft your ears will willingly purfue
Thro' each glad circumftance.   Firft, Monarch, learn,
The Roman troop is fled.

M O D R E D.

             Great Gods, we thank ye!

C A R A C T A C U S.

Fought they not ere they fled ? Oh tell me all.

B A R D.

Silent, as night, we pac'd up yonder hill,
While hid beneath its facrificial pall,
Did fleep our holy fire, nor faw the air,
'Till to that pafs we came, where whilom BRUTE
Planted his five hoar altars.   Inftant there,
We cloth'd each rocky pile with livid flame.
Near each a white-rob'd Druid, whofe ftern voice
Thunder'd deep execrations on the foe.
Now wak'd our horrid fymphony, now all
Our harps terrific rang : Mean while the grove
Trembled, the altars fhook, and thro' our ranks
Our facred fifters rufh'd with funeral brands,
Hurl'd round with menacing fury.   On they rufh'd
In fierce and frantic mood, as is their wont
Amid the magic rites, they do to NIGHT
In their deep dens below.   Motions like thefe
Were never dar'd before in open air !

M O D R E D.

Did I not fay, we had a pow'r within us,
That might appall ev'n Romans ?

B A R D.

                   And it did.
They ftood aghaft, and to our vollied darts
Scarce rais'd a warding fhield.   The facred trumpet
Then rent the air, and inftant at the fignal
Rufh'd down ARVIRAGUS with all our vaffals :
A hot, but fhort-liv'd, conflict then enfu'd :
For foon they fled.   I faw the Romans fly,
Before I left the field.   C A R-

CARACTACUS.
My fon purfu'd?
BARD.
The Prince and ELIDURUS, like twin lions,
Did fide by fide engage. Death feem'd to guide
Their fwords, no ftroke fell fruitlefs, every wound
Gave him a victim.
CARACTACUS.
Far did they purfue?
BARD.
Ev'n to the fhips: For I defcry'd the rout,
Far as the twilight gleam would aid my fight.
CARACTACUS.
Now, thanks to the bright ftar that rul'd his birth;
Yes, he will foon return to claim my bleffing,
And he fhall have it pour'd in tears of joy
On his bold breaft! methought I heard a ftep:
Is it not his?
BARD.
'Tis fome of our own train,
And as I think, they lead fix Romans captive.

SCENE III.
MODRED, CARACTACUS, CAPTIVES.
CHORUS.
CARACTACUS.
They feem of bold demeanor, and have helms,
That fpeak them leaders.
MODRED.
Bear them to the cavern.
CARACTACUS.
But while they live, treat them as men fhould men,
And not as Rome treats Britain. [*Exeunt Captives.*

SCENE

S C E N E IV.
EVELINA, CARACTACUS, MODRED,
C H O R U S.
E V E L I N A.

       O My father,
Support me, take me trembling to your arms ;
All is not well. Ah me, my fears o'ercome me !
C A R A C T A C U S.
What means my child ?
E V E L I N A.
      Alas ! we are betray'd.
Ev'n now as wandring in yon eaftern grove
I call'd the Gods to aid us, the dread found
Of many hafty fteps did meet mine ear :
This way they preft.
C A R A C T A C U S.
     Daughter, thy fears are vain.
E V E L I N A.
Methought I faw the flame of lighted brands,
And what did glitter to my dazzled fight,
Like fwords and helms.
C A R A C T A C U S.
     All, all the feeble coinage
Of maiden fear.
E V E L I NA
    Nay, if mine ear miftook not,
I heard the traitor's voice, who that way 'fcap'd,
Calling to arms.
C A R A C T A C U S.
    Away with idle terrors !
Know, thy brave brother's helm is crown'd with conqueft,
Our foes are fled, their leaders are our captives.
Smile, my lov'd child, and imitate the fun,
That rifes ruddy from behind yon Oaks
To hail him victor.

   I   MODRED.

MODRED.

That the rifing Sun !
O horror ! horror ! facrilegious fires
Devour our groves: They blaze, they blaze ! Oh found
The trump again; recall the Prince, or all
Is loft.

CARACTACUS.

Druid, where is thy fortitude ?
Do not I live ? Is not this holy fword
Firm in my grafp ? I will preferve your groves.
Britons, I go: Let thofe that dare die nobly,
Follow my ftep.   [*Exit Caractacus.*

EVELINA.

Oh whither does he go ?
Return, return : Ye holy men, ' recall him.
What is his arm againft a hoft of Romans ?
Oh I have loft a father !

MODRED.

Ruthlefs Gods !
Ye take away our fouls : A general panic
Reigns thro' the grove. Oh fly, my brethren, fly
To aid the King, fly to preferve your altars !
Alas ! 'tis all in vain ; our fate is fixt.
Look there, look there, thou miferable maid !
Behold thy bleeding brother.

SCENE V.

ARVIRAGUS, ELIDURUS, EVELINA, MODRED, CHORUS.

ARVIRAGUS.

Thanks, good youth !
Safe haft thou brought me to that holy fpot,
Where I did wifh to die. I would drag out
This life, tho' at fome coft of throbs and pangs,
Juft long enough to claim my father's bleffing,

And

And figh my laft breath in my fifter's arms.——
And here fhe kneels, poor maid ! all dumb with grief,
Reftrain thy forrow, gentleft EVELINA !
True, thou doft fee me bleed : I bleed to death.

E V E L I N A.

Say'ft thou to death ? O Gods ! the barbed fhaft
Is buried in his breaft. Yes, he muft die;
And I, alas ! am doom'd to fee him die.
Where are your healing arts, ye holy men ?
Pluck me but out this fhaft, ftanch but this blood,
And I will call down bleffings on your heads
With fuch a fervency—alas ! ye cannot,
Then let me beg you on my bended knee, .
Give to my mis'ry fome chill opiate drug
May fhut up all my fenfes.——Yes, good Fathers,
Mingle the potion fo, that it may kill me
Juft at the inftant this poor languifher
Heaves his laft figh.

A R V I R A G U S.

Talk not thus wildly, Sifter,

Think on our father's age———

E V E L N A.

Alas ! my Brother !

We have no father now ; or if we have,
He is a captive.

A R V I R A G U S.

Captive ! O my wound !

It ftings me now—But is it fo ? [*Turning to the Chorus.*

M O D R E D.

Alas !

We know no more, fave that he fallied fingle
To meet the foe, whofe unexpected hoft
Round by the eaft had wound their fraudful march,
And fir'd our groves.

E L I-

ELIDURUS.

O fatal, fatal valour!
Then is he feiz'd, or flain.

ARVIRAGUS.

Too fure he is!
Druid, not half the Romans met our fwords;
We found the fraud too late.: the reft are yonder.

MODRED.

How could they gain the pafs?

ARVIRAGUS.

The wretch, that fled
That way, return'd, conducting half their powers;
And—But thy pardon, youth, I will not wound thee,
He is thy brother.

ELIDURUS.

Thus my honeft fword
Shall force the blood from the detefted heart,
That holds alliance with him.

ARVIRAGUS.

Elidurus!
Hold, on our friendfhip, hold. Thou noble youth,
Look on this innocent maid. She muft to Rome,
Captive to Rome. Thou feeft warm life flow from me,
Ere long fhe'll have no brother. Heav'n's my witnefs,
I do not wifh, that thou fhould'ft live the flave
Of Rome: But yet fhe is my fifter.

ELIDURUS.

Prince!
Thou urgeft that, might make me drag an age
In fetters worfe than Roman. I will live,
And while I live————

SCENE VI.

Enter BARD.

Fly to your caverns, Druids!
The grove's befet around. The chief approaches.

CHORUS.

MODRED.

Let him approach, we will confront his pride;
The Seer that rules amid the groves of Mona
Has not to fear his fury. What tho' age
Slacken our finews; what tho' fhield and fword
Give not their iron aid to guard our body;
Yet virtue arms our foul, and 'gainft that panoply
What 'vails the rage of robbers? Let him come.

ARVIRAGUS.

I faint apace.—Ye venerable Men,
If ye can fave this body from pollution,
If ye can tomb me in this facred place,
I truft ye will. I fought to fave thefe groves,
And, fruitlefs tho' I fought, fome grateful Oak,
I truft, will fpread its reverential gloom
O'er my pale afhes—Ah! that pang was death!
My fifter, Oh!——   [*Dies.*

ELIDURUS.

                    She faints! Ah raife her! ——

EVELINA.

                                        Yes,

Now he is dead. I felt his fpirit go
In a cold figh, and as it paft, methought
It paus'd a while, and trembled on my lips!
Take me not from him: Breathlefs as he is,
He is my brother ftill, and if the Gods
Do pleafe to grace him with fome happier being,
They ne'er can give to him a fonder fifter.

MODRED.

Brethren, furround the corfe, and, ere the foe
Approaches, chaunt with meet folemnity
That grateful dirge your dying champion claims.
                                        [*Symphony.*

MADOR.

Lo! where incumbent o'er the fhade
Rome's rav'ning eagle bows her beaked head!

                                        Yet

Yet while a moment fate affords;
While yet a moment freedom stays;
That moment, which outweighs
Eternity's unmeasur'd hoards,
Shall Mona's grateful Bards employ
To hymn their godlike Hero to the sky,

Second B A R D.
A I R.

Radiant Ruler of the day!
  Pause upon thy orb sublime,
Bid this awful moment stay,
  Bind it on the brow of time;
While Mona's trembling echoes sigh
To strains that trill when heroes die.

Fourth B A R D.
A I R.

Hear our harps, in accents slow,
Breathe the dignity of woe,
Solemn notes that pant, and pause,
While the last majestic close,
In diapason deep is drown'd;
Notes that Mona's harps should sound.

Third B A R D.
A I R.

See our tears, in sober shower,
O'er this shrine of glory pour;
Holy tears, by Virtue shed,
That embalm the valiant dead;
In these our sacred song we steep,
Tears that Mona's Bards should weep.

T R I O.

Radiant Ruler! hear us call
  Blessings on the godlike Youth,
Who dar'd to fight, who dar'd to fall,
  For Britain, Freedom, and for Truth.

His

His dying groan, his parting sigh,
Was music for the Gods on high;
'Twas Valor's hymn to Liberty.

MADOR.

Ring out ye mortal strings !
Answer thou heav'nly harp instinct with spirit all,
That o'er ANDRASTES' throne self-warbling swings.
There, where ten thousand spheres, in measur'd chime,
Roll their majestic melodies along,
Thou guid'st the thundering song,
Pois'd on thy jaspar arch sublime.
Yet shall thy heav'nly accents deign
To mingle with our mortal strain,
And Heav'n and Earth unite, in chorus high,
While Freedom wafts her champion to the sky.

Full CHORUS.

ANDRASTES' heav'nly harp shall deign
To mingle with our mortal strain,
And Heav'n and Earth unite, in chorus high,
While Freedom wafts her champion to the sky.

SCENE VII.

AULUS DIDIUS, MODRED, EVELINA, ELI-DURUS, CHORUS.

AULUS DIDIUS.

Ye bloody priests,
Behold we burst on your infernal rites,
And bid you pause. Instant restore our soldiers,
Nor hope that Superstition's ruthless step
Shall wade in Roman gore. Ye savage men,
Did not our laws give licence to all faiths,
We would o'erturn your altars, headlong heave
These shapeless symbols of your barbarous Gods,
And let the golden sun into your caves.

MODRED.

MODRED.

Servant of CÆSAR, has thine impious tongue
Spent the black venom of its blafphemy?
It has: then take our curfes on thy head,
Ev'n his fell curfes, who doth reign in Mona,
Vicegerent of thofe Gods thy pride infults.

AULUS DIDIUS.

Bold prieft, I fcorn thy curfes, and thyfelf.
Soldiers, go fearch the caves, and free the prifoners.
Take heed ye feize CARACTACUS alive.
Arreft yon youth; load him with heavieft irons;
He fhall to CÆSAR anfwer for his crime.

ELIDURUS.

I ftand prepar'd to triumph in my crime.

AULUS DIDIUS.

'Tis well, proud boy——Look to the beauteous maid
                                        [To the foldiers.
That, 'tranc'd in grief, bends o'er yon bleeding corfe:
Refpect her forrows.

EVELINA.

                    Hence ye barbarous men,
Ye fhall not take him welt'ring thus in blood,
To fhew at Rome what Britifh virtue was.
Avaunt! The breathlefs body that ye touch
Was once ARVIRAGUS!

AULUS DIDIUS.

                    Fear us not, Princefs!
We reverence the dead.

MODRED.

                    Would too to heav'n
Ye reverenc'd the Gods but ev'n enough
Not to debafe with Slavery's cruel chain
What they created free.

AULUS DIDIUS.

                    The Romans fight
Not to enflave, but humanize the world.

MODRED.

MODRED.

Go to, we will not parley with thee, Roman:
Inſtant pronounce our doom.

AULUS DIDIUS.

Hear it, and thank us:
This once our clemency ſhall ſpare your groves,
If, at our call, ye yield the Britiſh King:
Yet learn, when next ye aid the foes of CÆSAR,
That each old Oak, whoſe ſolemn gloom ye boaſt,
Shall bow beneath our axes.

MODRED.

Be they blaſted
Whene'er their ſhade forgets to ſhelter virtue.

SCENE VIII.

Enter BARD.

Mourn, Mona, mourn. CARACTACUS is captive!
And doſt thou ſmile, falſe Roman? Do not think
He fell an eaſy prey. Know, ere he yielded,
Thy braveſt veterans bled. He too, thy Spy,
The baſe Brigantian Prince, hath ſeal'd his fraud
With death. The brave CARACTACUS himſelf
Seiz'd his falſe throat; and as he gave the blow
Indignant thunder'd, "Thus is my laſt ſtroke
" The ſtroke of juſtice." Numbers then oppreſt him:
I ſaw the ſlave that cowardly behind
Pinion'd his arms; I ſaw the ſacred ſword
Writh'd from his graſp; I ſaw, what now ye ſee,
Inglorious ſight! thoſe barbarous bonds upon him.

SCENE IX.

CARACTACUS, AULUS DIDIUS, MODRED, CHORUS, &c.

CARACTACUS.

Romans, methinks the malice of your tyrant
Might furniſh heavier chains. Old as I am,

K

Truſt

Truſt me, I've ſtrength to bear the weightieſt load
Injuſtice dares impoſe.——

           Proud-creſted ſoldier! [*To Didius.*
Say, doſt thou read leſs terror on my brow
Than when thou met'ſt me in the fields of war,
Heading my nations? No: my free-born ſoul
Has ſcorn ſtill left to ſparkle thro' theſe eyes,
And frown defiance on thee.—Is it thus!

                [*Seeing his ſon's body.*
Then I'm indeed a captive.   Mighty Gods!
My ſoul, my ſoul ſubmits: Patient it bears
The pond'rous load of grief ye heap upon it,
And is the ſad tame thing it ought to be,
Coopt in a ſervile body.

A U L U S   D I D I U S.
          Droop not, King.
When CLAUDIUS, the great maſter of the world,
Shall hear the noble ſtory of thy valour,
His pity——

C A R A C T A C U S.
        Can a Roman pity, ſoldier?
And if he can, Gods! muſt a Briton bear it?
ARVIRAGUS, my bold, my breathleſs boy,
Thou haſt eſcap'd ſuch pity; thou art free.
Here in high Mona ſhall thy noble limbs
Reſt in a noble grave; Poſterity
Shall pile ſepulchral ſtones upon thy corſe:
Whilſt mine——

A U L U S   D I D I U S.
        The morn doth haſten our departure,
Prepare thee, King, to go: A fav'ring gale
Now ſwells our ſails.

C A R A C T A C U S.
        Inhuman that thou art!
Doſt thou deny a moment for a father
To ſhed a few warm tears o'er his dead ſon?

I

I tell thee, Chief, this act might claim a life
To do that office duly. Cruel man!
And thou denieft me moments. Be it fo.
I know you Romans weep not for your children;
Ye triumph o'er your tears, and think it valour:
I triumph in my tears. Yes, beft-lov'd boy;
Yes, I can weep, can tear thefe few grey hairs,
The only honours war and age have left me.
Ah, fon! thou might'ft have rul'd o'er many nations,
As did thy royal anceftry: but I,
Rafh that I was, ne'er knew the golden curb
Difcretion hangs on brav'ry; elfe perchance
Thefe men that faften fetters on thy father
Had fu'd to him for peace, and claim'd his friendfhip.

AULUS DIDIUS.

But thou waft ftill implacable to Rome,
And fcorn'd her friendfhip.

CARACTACUS *ftarting up from the body.*

Soldier, I had arms,

Had neighing fteeds to whirl my iron cars,
Had wealth, dominion. Doft thou wonder, Roman,
I fought to fave them? What if CÆSAR aims
To lord it univerfal o'er the world,
Shall the world tamely crouch at CÆSAR's footftool?

AULUS DIDIUS.

Read in thy fate our anfwer. Yet if fooner
Thy pride had yielded——

CARACTACUS.

Thank thy Gods, I did not.

Had it been fo, the glory of thy mafter,
Like my misfortunes, had been fhort and trivial,
Oblivion's ready prey: Now, after ftruggling
Nine years, and that right bravely, 'gainft a tyrant,
I am his flave to treat as feems him good:
If cruelly, 'twill be an eafy tafk
To bow a wretch, alas, how bow'd already!

K 2

Down

Down to the dust: If well, his clemency
May shine in honour's annals, and adorn
Himself: it boots not me. Look there! look there!
The slave that shot that dart kill'd ev'ry hope
Of lost CARACTACUS! Arise, my daughter.
Alas! poor Prince! art thou too in vile fetters?

                                        [To Elidurus.

Come hither, Youth: Be thou to me a son,
To her a brother. Thus with trembling arms
I lead you forth: Children, we go to Rome.
Weep'ft thou, my girl? I prithee hoard thy tears
For the sad meeting of thy captive mother:
For we have much to tell her. Think'ft thou, maid,
Her gentlenefs can bear that tale, and live?

                                [Pointing to his dead Son.

And yet she muft. O Gods, I grow a talker!
Grief and old age are ever full of words:
But I'll be mute. Adieu, ye holy men!
Yet one look more.—Now lead us hence for ever.

A Dead March.

During which CARACTACUS, EVELINA, *and* ELIDURUS
are led off by ROMANS.

T H E E N D.

www.ingramcontent.com/pod-product-compliance
Lightning Source LLC
Chambersburg PA
CBHW032355020726
47499CB00008B/2757